BLAIRE SQUISCOLL

The Frankfurt Kabuff

A Beatrice Deft (Comic Erotic) Thriller

First published by Kabuff Books 2019

First edition

ISBN: 978-1-9993676-1-9

This book was professionally typeset on Reedsy. Find out more at reedsy.com

Contents

CHAPTER EINS

Beatrice sipped her Negroni and took a long drag of her cigarette, leaving a bright red lipstick stain on the filter. Frankfurt was unseasonably warm, with hot sunlight beating through the autumn leaves. Bodies blurred past, but she paid them no heed. Beatrice wasn't here for anyone but herself. The chicken shop incident had wrung her dry.

In the distance she heard sirens, the European nee-nah that she had found so amusing on her first trip here... how many years ago now? Too many to count; how had she become so jaded at the age of only thirty-two, and a Scorpio at that.

The solicitous young waiter stopped at the end of her table. His chiseled jaw moved as he spoke, his words English but his accent distinctly teutonic. "May I bring you anuzza drink, madam?" His bright blue eyes sparkled down at her, the hint of a flirtatious smile played at the corners of his lips.

She assessed him coolly. Once, before the chicken shop, she wouldn't have hesitated to twinkle back at him, make a flirtatious joke even. But some spark inside her had gone out, and remained unlit for months now. His smile faded suddenly and she wondered if a shadow had passed across her face. She tried a smile of her own, but it felt more like a baring of teeth.

"Madam?" he asked again.

"Just the bill," she said abruptly. "And where can I buy more cigarettes and red lipstick?"

She wondered why he had given her a second glance. Her enormous blue eyes were hidden behind sunglasses, and all her lipstick had come off while chain smoking. Her luggage had gone missing and she was still in the clingy tunic and leggings she had slept in on the long flight from Australia. The Negroni was her first meal of the day.

The waiter smiled. "If you give me your room number, I will charge it to your account. And the shops are zat way." He indicated with a shrug of his well-developed shoulder.

"Five-oh-seven," she said. Then she jabbed her cigarette at the crowded gathering she could see across the road. "What is going on over there?"

"Die Buchmesse, Madam. The Frankfurt Book Fair. Do you like books?"

She shrugged. "I did. Once." She pushed back her chair and pulled her bag over her shoulder, and went upstairs to her room. She didn't notice the quiet elderly man at the next table, who had carefully noted her room number.

CHAPTER ZWEI

Klopf klopf!

Beatrice jerked awake, her body working more quickly than her mind. She felt the touch of 100% Egyptian cotton on her skin, then the sound of another loud knock. Frankfurt, she thought. Autumn. But how long had she been asleep?

She jumped up, pulling the sheets around her as she opened the door a crack. A scent of musky cologne hit her as her jetlagged eyes appraised brilliantined stubble.

"Madam," said the porter, gesturing by his hip. Beatrice lowered her gaze to a black suitcase. Hers.

"Ja, it has arrived." He gestured his dimpled chin over her shoulder, into the room. "Do you want me to bring it in for you?"

She dragged her hand through her jet black hair, lifting her eyes back up to meet his. Only the sheet stood between her and the porter. Then she remembered throwing clothes into the suitcase in her Melbourne home, swearing to herself she would never look upon the sinsterly bright facade of that chicken shop again.

"No... not now," she breathed, taking the handle of the bag and dragging it into the room, closing the door behind her.

She leaned back heavily against the door, casting her eye around the room. The empty cigarette packet stared back, its rumpled cellophane taunting her. She closed her eyes for a second, then swooped down within one agile movement to unzip her luggage. She grabbed her toiletry bag and strode towards the shower.

Ten seconds later Beatrice emerged, refreshed. She spilled clothes out of the suitcase, strewing them across the luxurious carpet, a sea of black on the ocean of russet-green. A shapeless yet stylish black dress topped the pile. She threw it on, laced up her black leather boots to the thigh with red ribbons, and headed out into the fading evening light.

**

The smell of piss hit her first. One street had led to another until she found herself in a cluttered laneway. Men in

5

stained sleeping bags called out to her. Beatrice hated all forms of economic inequality.

"Hey, Australian lady," a rough voice hailed her. "Got any cigarettes?"

She was flush with cigarettes; stocking up had been her reason for this long walk in the first place. She strode over, boots clinking on cobbles and dodging construction paraphernalia. She fished in her Allen & Unwin tote bag, and withdrew a Camel, which he took gratefully.

He pointed at the bag. "You here for the publisher party?"

She shrugged. "I suppose I could. Where is it?"

He pointed with his Camel at the Red Russian pole-dancing club. "Down there. Thanks for the cigarette."

"No problem."

A dark-haired Frankfurter at the door gave her a quick glance and ushered her in. She found herself walking along a crimson corridor, surrounded by erotic art. She followed it to a steep staircase, into a womb-like space below. In the tiny dark room, Primal Scream's "Loaded" blasted from tinny speakers. Beatrice was unexpectedly charmed. Everywhere she looked, suited men and chicly dressed women smiled, talked, and bobbed along to the music. Genuine enthusiasm animated their gestures and expressions. Once, she had been this optimistic. She wondered if she could be again.

As she moved towards the bar, she noted with a frown that a tall, dark-haired man with well-developed biceps, a thick baton, and the word POLIZEI emblazoned across his jacket, glowered from the corner of the room. Why would they need a police officer here? Everybody seemed so nice.

While Beatrice waited for her Negroni, drumming her dark red fingernails on the bar, she found herself pressed against two older men in blue suits, as they shouted to be heard over the music.

At first she could only hear snatches of their conversation, words that didn't seem to belong in this happy, carefree space. "Threat of violence" "mitigate against the danger" "guns" "bombs".

Even if she knew this wasn't her problem, she was intrigued enough to lean closer.

Then, in an oddly long gap between songs, one of their voices reached her ears as clear as a bell.

"Something terrible is going to happen at the Book Fair

tomorrow."

CHAPTER DREI

Beatrice's lungs heaved in the night-time air. Was there no escape from danger, even thousands of miles and two seasons away from Australia?

A soft step sounded in the laneway behind her. She span round, instinctively tightening her knuckles.

It was the tall policeman from the party. Her breath pumped around her breast as she took in flawless tanned skin, straight nose, full lips.

"Are you alright?" His voice was deep, concerned. Warm brown eyes fixed on hers. "I saw you running out of the club."

"I... two men were discussing an attack, bombs, at the Book Fair... I needed air."

The man shifted his weight. "Ach so. Everyone is talking about this book. It is the book of the fair, I hear. Are you a publisher?"

Beatrice looked down at the cobbles before replying. "Why were you at the party? Is there a security issue?"

"Nein, nein. One of the Ambassadors wanted to come. He loves books. And parties."

"And Ferrero Rocher?" she riposted.

The policeman smiled, showing a set of perfect white teeth." 'Something like that. Listen, my shift has finished. Can I walk you to your hotel? It's late, and this area..."

"Officer... what's your name?"

"Polizeiobermeister Schorle. But call me Caspian. I am off duty now."

"Caspian..." She rolled the letters round her mouth like a long cooling drink after a hot day. "Sure, why not. If you're heading in my direction."

***

Beatrice threw off her dress and climbed onto the bed, clutching the small business card that Caspian had thrust into her hand. When they'd parted at the hotel entrance, she'd thought for a moment about inviting him in for a nightcap. She'd felt something kindling inside of her.

Instead, she'd asked for his number. She laughed as she remembered him bashfully pointing to his shapely uniformed shoulder. 6969. Who says numbers aren't sexy, she thought. Three stars, as well.

She scrutinised the card he'd given her: a red boot, a shop name and a Frankfurt address. As they parted, he'd told her that if she needed him, to go to this shop. "My aunt - Tante Fran - she will help," he said earnestly.

Shaking her head, a wry smile playing on her lips, she sank back into the feather pillows. For the first time in months she let her body relax.

As she reached over to turn off the bedside light, she noticed an envelope propped up by the telephone. She grabbed it, feeling its weight and texture. 300gsm minimum.

An elaborate cursive script read B.D., Room 507. Startled, she sat up, and tore open the envelope:

Sehr geehrte Frau Deft:

Never have we met, but many years ago I knew

your mother. When you receive this, whatever time
of the day or night, please call me. I need your help.
I am in Room 233.

K.W.

Beatrice's heart accelerated. Her hand moved towards the phone. She thought about last time someone needed her help, and pulled her fingers back sharply. But he'd known her dear, late mother; he might have memories of her.

***

Down in the hotel bar, the Bosendorfer tinkled and low conversations hummed. The light was dim, but she spotted an elderly, bearded man in a sharp blue suit, nursing a Campari and soda and gazing at her intently. She strode over and thrust out her hand.

"Are you Kurt Weidenfeld?"

"Sit, sit," he said. "Ah, you are ferry image of your mother."

Beatrice smiled. She had been told this before, and it never failed to delight her.

A cloud moved across his face. "I could always count on your mother to care for those in danger."

Beatrice's heart twisted. Her mother had pushed a young boy's pram out of the way of an oncoming bus, only to feel its full force herself. It had been Beatrice's tenth birthday. "Caring can be dangerous," she said, snapping her fingers for the waiter.

His tone became stern. "So can not caring, mein Liebchen."

She sighed. "You'd best explain yourself."

"I am a publisher of left-wing philosophy. For the past month I have been receiving threats from White Storm, a network of newspapers and zines dedicated to reviving the worst ideas and policies of the twentieth century."

Beatrice gulped. "Nazis?" The waiter arrived with her Negroni. Clearly she already had a reputation.

Kurt waited for them to be alone again, then spoke, "They have warned me, and others like me, to stay away from Frankfurt. They want it all to themselves. They say, if we cannot have die Buchmesse as our exclusive platform, then they will destroy it."

13

Beatrice interjected. "But Frankfurt Book Fair is about the exchange of ideas!"

"I know, Liebchen. But there are those who would seek to control it. If I turn up tomorrow, I am in danger. My small press requires international rights sales to survive. While I am in meetings, can you be my eyes and ears?"

She hesitated. Last time she had got involved in somebody else's problems, it had all gone horribly wrong. Her eyes misted over as she remembered...

CHAPTER VIER

Cold drizzle falls through the gum trees and settles around my shoulders like a shawl. Crickets chirrup and a possum scampers across the electricity wires. I turn the key in the lock of our Federation-style townhouse.

"Callum?" I call.

"Back here." I hear in his voice that he's in good spirits.

I find him in our cupboard-sized kitchen. The red wine is open. He hasn't waited for me.

"The meeting went well then?"

He rounds the table and kisses me distractedly. "Allen & Unwin have agreed to distribute us. Florencia Intelligensia books will be in all reputable bookstores!"

"Congratulations." His dream come true.

"Here's a tote bag they gave me. You can have it. You're always carrying around those old books you love so much."

"They're called classics, Callum, and they are changing my students' lives."

"It's just high school," Callum says. "They'll stop reading when they graduate, just like the other sheeple in this godforsaken Melbourne suburb."

I bite my lip. We've been over this ground before.

I place the bag from Kev's Hot Chicken on the table. "I got us dinner." He hands me a glass of wine. "A real celebration then."

"Amina served me. I'm so proud of her. Her family came here with nothing as refugees from Sudan, and now she's topping my English class as well as holding down a part-time job. She seemed a bit tired, though. I hope nothing is troubling her."

"You worry too much about other people, Bea."

"But she's our next-door-neighbour."

He doesn't respond, tearing into juicy flesh with one hand, while the other adjusts his man bun.

Callum changes the topic and we chat over dinner, mostly about his supply-chain logistics. The wine disappears quickly. While he is getting a second bottle from our wine rack, I hear the slam of a car door and raised voices.

"What is that?" I say, rising from my chair.

"Leave it, Bea," Callum says.

I walk outside to the paved courtyard, where the last few bougainvillea flowers cling sadly to the dripping vine. I can see a sliver of the street. Two white men, broad across the shoulders, loom over Amina, whose slight body is flexed in a posture of defiance.

I strain to hear, but nothing comes to me clearly. Then one of the men — I recognise him as Kev — shakes his fist and shouts at Amina over the deepening rain.

"You need to forget what you saw!"

CHAPTER FÜNF

The sun beat down on Frankfurt. Beatrice paced the streets, the skyscrapers of the banking district overshadowing her, reminding her of Melbourne. She wanted to forget what she'd seen... but she couldn't. She'd come to Germany to escape, but Herr Wiedenfeld wanted her eyes and ears.

She turned into the cobbles of the New Old Town. Tourists were queuing for ice creams. Her head throbbed. She'd brought the wrong clothes for this unseasonably warm weather.

"New shoes," she whispered to herself, pulling the business card that Caspian had given her out of the thick fabric of her dress pocket.

The shop front that Google maps had directed her to hadn't been decorated in decades, red paint flaking from its woodwork. But the modest window display had some surprisingly stylish footwear. A bell tinkled as she pushed the door open.

She trailed her fingers across the shelves, picking out some heels. She slipped her right foot in, revelling in the caress of its insole against her skin. This was a heel that meant business.

"Zat is the Schuh for you," a soft female voice sounded.

Beatrice jumped, looking to the shadows at the back of the shop. "Is that..." she hesitated, "Tante Fran?"

"Ja," replied the women. "And you must be Beatrice, am I correct? I will get you the left shoe."

Tante Fran emerged from the cupboard, holding the matching heel. Beatrice could see in her face Caspian's full lips and deep eyes.

"Thank you. I'll take them."

Tante Fran put both shoes into a cardboard box and a bright red bag.

"Caspian told me you are interested in ze structural inequalities of society," Tante Fran said as Beatrice held out her credit card. "Though not how beautiful you are. Would you like to join our reading group while you are visiting? We meet every Wednesday. We're on Marcuse's Eros and

Civilisation. Or on Fridays we paint slogans..."

Beatrice clasped her shoes to her chest, unsure how to reply.

The tinkling of the bell broke the heavy silence of the shop. "Caspian, Neffe!" called Tante Fran.

Beatrice span round. Caspian's broad silhouette was framed in the door. Deep in her pelvis, she felt the sensation that had evaded her for months.

CHAPTER SECHS

Caspian's eyes met Beatrice's for a moment of smouldering intensity. A charge passed between him and her, but then he abruptly turned away to address Tante Fran, although his use of heavily accented English indicated he wanted to include Beatrice.

"I had to come and find you. White Storm is gathering at die Buchmesse!"

Tante Fran's face took on a resolute expression. "I will phone the book club immediately!"

Caspian turned to Beatrice. "I'm sorry. You tried to warn me at the party. I was wrong to dismiss you."

"White Storm?" Beatrice said. "An old friend of my mother's, Kurt Weidenfeld, told me he had been receiving threats from them."

"Kurt Weidenfeld! The famous publisher of left-wing

philosophy?" Tante Fran exclaimed. Her voice softened. "Kurt and I have known each other for many years."

"He asked me to be his eyes and ears in meetings, but I didn't want to get involved."

"But we must involve ourselves in the lives of others who need our help," Caspian said firmly. "That is what it is to be truly human."

Beatrice felt warmth rise in her breast; he shared her values.

Then Caspian said, "Come."

A few moments later, they were hailing a cab to the Book Fair. In the back of the cab, she could feel the heat from his body radiating towards her. His muscular arms were tightly crossed, making his shoulders bulge against his dark blue uniform. She wondered what kind of books he read.

"You are going to the Book Fair?" said the cab driver. "I have an idea for a book I've always wanted to write since I arrived here from Turkey."

Beatrice had a twinge; she had no commissioning power as she didn't work for a publisher, but she wanted to know this man's story. She was interested in every human being. "I have little influence in the publishing world," she said, "but go on."

"It's David Nicholls' *One Day* meets Harry Potter. Two young wizards meet on the same day, July 31st, every year, for 20 years. It will appeal to young adults around the world!"

Beatrice was impressed with the commercial potential of this idea, which could reach readers across class, race and gender divides. "You have a talent," she said. "May I pass your pitch on to my friend, Kurt Weidenfeld?"

"The famed philosophical left-wing publisher? Of course!"

They pulled up outside the Messe. Red and white flags fluttered in the sunshine, small stall holders were selling secondhand books, German sausages, beer, and pretzels. Caspian took her through a special side entrance, nodding to a police officer who turned her lips up in a smile in return, and said something to him in German. Inside Hall Four, row upon row of publishers stalls greeted her gaze. Some of the stands were very small, but others were colossal, like fortresses. Everywhere Beatrice looked, there were posters of forthcoming titles and rows of books. She had never seen so many. Men in blue suits milled around. Several police officers patrolled the corridors, their guns and batons conspicuous.

Caspian laid a firm hand on her upper arm. She was surprised by the heat on her skin. "I must go to meet with my commander," he said. "You'll find Kurt in row B." He fixed her in his magnetic gaze. "Be careful."

"I will," Beatrice said, and hurried off to find Kurt's stand. Towards the end of row B, she discovered him wedged between other small, left-wing publishers and, surprisingly, a greeting card manufacturer. The Linksphilosophie Verlag sign was pinned to the wall behind his desk, where he sat in a meeting with a doe-eyed young woman, selling his rights.

When he saw Beatrice, he leapt to his feet. "Mein Liebchen!" he exclaimed. "I thought you would not come."

"I was persuaded," she said meaningfully. "But first, could you direct me to the ladies room?" It had been a long cab ride.

"Behind the Google Play stand," he said, gesturing, then sat down to return to his meeting.

Beatrice strode towards the stand. As she walked past Google Play, she saw a plain white wall with a gap in it, and assumed this must be the way to the toilet. She stepped through and was shocked to find that the gloss and colour of the Hall had disappeared. This space was different. Vast, bare concrete floor and rudimentary plywood greeted her eyes. Were there not enough publishers to fill the hall? What was happening to the industry? Her steps echoed as she found her way to the toilets, still thinking.

She pulled open a door, but it wasn't a washroom. It was a cupboard, the size of a small store room, with coats, bags, and trays of mineral water. Shelving lined the back wall, and held cardboard boxes and odd shapes wrapped in canvas. Before she had a moment to realise she was in the wrong place, a woman's voice called shrilly in German. She turned to see a tall, strapping, blonde woman glaring at her. The woman, seeing Beatrice was uncomprehending, marched over and slammed the cupboard door.

She switched to English. "Don't go in there and don't come back here again. You'll be sorry if you do."

CHAPTER SIEBEN

Beatrice backed away, her heels catching on the rough concrete. The blonde stood, arms crossed, legs akimbo, blocking the cupboard door.

The woman's unblinking eyes locked on Beatrice's, and the two women stood still for a second. Tumbleweeds crossed the empty floor.

Beatrice felt a vibration at her hip, and dropped her gaze as she took her phone from her dress pocket to scrutinise the screen. "CASPIAN message," it read. She felt a tightening in her body as she swiped:

```
KW asks me to inform you that the location of his
    next meeting has been altered. Meet him at the
    Executive Club. There are good women's
    facilities, he says.
```

Beatrice's fingers hovered over the reply box, contemplating what to reply. The phone thrilled again in her hand.

Cx

A rush swept through her. Without pondering the consequences, she thumbed:

Bx

She lifted her eyes from the intimate glow of the screen.

The woman was gone. The door of the cupboard had melted into the plywood facade.

***

Beatrice slicked lipstick over her mouth, ran her fingers through her hair, and met her own eyes in the Executive Club mirror, smiling at her appearance. The young woman guarding the entrance to the Club had frowned as she had searched on an iPad for Kurt's meeting.

"Ja, I have it. He is meeting with ze boss." Her eyebrows lifted, but her expression became no more friendly. "Let me take you," the woman said, gesturing into the dimly lit interior of the Club. "The toilets are that way if you need them."

Beatrice emerged from the toilets, and the young woman weaved her through low tables surrounded by grey up-holstered club chairs. Fringing separated out areas at the sides of the Club. Men and the occasional woman talked in hushed tones, their monochrome outfits barely discernible against the grey and black.

They approached a table in one corner. Beatrice saw Kurt first, his frame – so debonair in the bar of hotel – crumpling towards a grey-haired man with his back to her. She noted the expensive cut of the grey-haired man's blue suit. A young woman was sitting passively between the two men, her hands clutching a notebook and pen, her blonde hair neatly tied into a ponytail. An empty chair sat opposite her.

Kurt noticed Beatrice's approach, and got to his feet with some effort, putting his hand gently to her elbow.

"Beatrice, Liebchen, thank you for coming... Let me intro-duce you..."

She looked down to the imposing face of the man with whom Kurt was meeting. He met her gaze impassively, and for a moment she thought he was going to refuse to take the hand which she had proffered to him. Then he clasped her hand in both of his, and she felt him pull her down into the fourth chair. The young woman opposite her did not lift her eyes from her notebook.

Kurt glanced between them. "Beatrice," he said, his voice low, "we are discussing the issue of White Storm."

The young woman wrote something down in her notebook.

'A drink, perhaps?' said the man. "I hear you take Negronis." He waved over the waitress from the bar.

"Just a tea," Beatrice said. She would need her wits around her for this conversation.

"As the Vice President of the Buchmesse, I am committed to freedom of speech." The Vice President's piercing blue eyes bored into her. "The robust exchange of ideas is our raison d'etre. But Herr Weidenfeld wants me to censor the fair."

The young woman reached forward and moved some pieces on the table. Beatrice realised it was a scale model of Hall 3.

"White Storm poses more than an ideological threat!" Kurt exclaimed. "The safety of exhibitors and visitors is at risk!"

The VP's impassive face remained so.

"What needs to happen before you will take this seriously?" Kurt's appeal was impassioned, but also weak, as if he knew he would not be listened to.

Beatrice bent down and looked closely at the model. She could see a small stand marked Linksphilosophie Verlag, and right opposite, a stand marked White Storm. And, at the back of that tiny cardboard stand, a tiny cardboard cupboard.

"I see you have noticed the Kabuff," the Vice President said.

"The what?"

"The Kabuff. A Kabuff is a cupboard, a cobwebby cupboard where things are hidden. Where unpleasant surprises may lurk. Have you not read Heinrich Mann?"

Beatrice felt a chill run through her. Was she being threatened? How much did he know?

"I didn't catch your name, Herr Vice President," she said coolly.

He handed her an embossed, heavy white card. Kristoff Wiel, Vice President for Intellectual Freedom, Frankfurt

31

Buchmesse. She tucked it into her purse.

"ACHTUNG!!!" It was Caspian! Standing at the entrance of the Executive Club, firmly gripping his lengthy baton. For a moment the room stood still as she appraised Caspian in action.

"Everybody needs to clear the room NOW. SCHNELL!"

No sooner were the words out of his mouth than a loud noise, like a gunshot, cracked through the air. A shocked silence gripped the room, before people started rushing for the exit. Half a dozen men and women in white shirts and caps were running through the main entrance. One of Caspian's fellow officers came in just behind them, his face swollen and his nose bleeding.

The young woman grabbed Beatrice's arms. "We must go. But find me later if you can. I have information for you." She slipped a business card into Beatrice's palm before melting into the crowd. Beatrice looked around wildly, her heart pumping. Where was Caspian? Where was Kristoff? More punches were being thrown in the melée. Beatrice pocketed the card, took Kurt's arm, and pushed him towards the exit.

CHAPTER ACHT

Beatrice slumped against the exterior wall of the Executive Club, the gold lettering of its signage mirroring back her still-sharp hairstyle. She wished she'd ordered that Negroni after all. Herr Weidenfeld was talking to a group of older women they had met in the Agora – Tante Fran's book club, she supposed – and Beatrice was alone. Alone, shaken, and desperate for answers. How did it all join together? The threats against the left wing publisher, the Kabuff and the blonde woman who guarded it, the small-scale model of the fair, Herr Vice President and the blonde woman with the notebook, the White Storm violence. Beatrice shuffled the business cards in her wallet. She was getting quite a collection. Her touch lingered on Caspian's card, tracing the embossed curves of his name and email address.

"You are craving a cigarette, perhaps?" The deep, startling voice interrupted her musings. No, Beatrice thought, she didn't crave cigarettes anymore. Odd. She looked up and into the eyes that had cast such a spell on her.

"You never did tell me what books you like to read, Caspian."

"Biographies, mostly."

Her breath hitched. Reading about those who had over-come obstacles to lead great and meaningful lives inspired her, too.

"You were impressive in there."

Caspian held her gaze for a few beats, then looked away in frustration. "It is not enough. They are toying with us. This was a distraction while they plan something else."

Before she knew it, she had reached out and taken his hand in hers. For a moment they stood there together against the exterior wall of the Executive Club, drawing mute comfort from each other's physical presence even while they worried about the future. Suddenly Beatrice snapped to attention.

"The Kabuff!" she cried. "There must be more to what is happening in that mysterious cupboard."

She put her hand up to Caspian's cheek. "I have to go and have another look. Keep messaging me, OK?"

Caspian's face dipped towards hers, his mouth electrifyingly close as he whispered, "I will." Then the contact was broken, and Beatrice strode off towards Hall 3.

***

As she turned down aisle B, Beatrice noticed Kurt was back at the Linksphilosophie Verlag stand, talking animatedly with his rights director, Adriana.

Kurt noticed Beatrice, and raised his hand to her. She lifted her finger to her lips, motioning him to silence. He nodded, swiftly, and went back to his conversation. The rights director was frowning at Kurt's gesticulations, and looking anxiously across the aisle at the austere stand opposite them. White Storm.

The stand was fronted by a man as broad as he was tall, his shiny blue suit and tie mirroring his gristly, misshapen face. He scowled at each passerby, who looked away and hurried onwards without meeting his eye. Behind him were none of the colourful displays of books featuring on the other stands in the aisle. Instead, there was a pile of newspapers, their typeface reminiscent of the 1930s. The back of the stand was covered with a black and white printed design of a crowd holding their right arms aloft, palms down.

Beatrice shivered. The image should be relegated to a high school history class, she thought.

Suddenly the printed crowd moved forward, and Beatrice wondered if jet lag had finally caught up with her. But then, she realised a door had opened in the back drop, shifting a portion of the picture of the crowd towards her. Behind the door, she glimpsed something. The Kabuff!

She stepped back quickly into the protection of the next-door stand, as a tall blonde emerged and closed the door quickly behind her. It was the strapping woman who had warned her away earlier from the cupboard in the concrete area. Beatrice watched as she locked the door, nodded to the man on the front of the stand, and handed him a small key before she marched off in the direction of the toilets.

Beatrice took a sharp intake of breath. She knew she had to get into the Kabuff.

She took out her phone and texted Kurt:

```
I am going to investigate White Storm's Kabuff.
    Ask Adriana to distract the oaf on the stand.
```

Kurt picked up his phone, then looked over to her, consternation on his face. She nodded, emphatically, and Kurt reluctantly whispered in the rights director's ear, who got up, smoothed her skirt, and crossed the aisle, shooting Beatrice a conspiratorial glance.

***

Beatrice waited five minutes, until she saw Adriana had managed to make the stand minder laugh, though it looked more like a contorted grimace. She dodged into the stand, and remembering the technique from a novel, twisted her hand into the minder's pocket, extracted the key without him noticing. She smiled to herself, thinking at last she had something to thank Dickens for, unlocked the door, and let herself into the Kabuff.

As she silently pulled the door behind her, darkness closed in. She used her hands to see, feeling coats, bags, bottles, and cardboard boxes. She moved forwards a step, and stubbed her toe. She swore under her breath, hoping her new shoe wasn't damaged, then remembered Tante Fran. With resolve, she switched on her phone's flashlight, and saw a trapdoor on the Kabuff floor.

***

The space underneath the Kabuff was dusty and cobwebby. Beatrice realised she must be in the ceiling space between floors. Shining her flashlight around her, she saw markings on the wooden uprights of the stands. Raised arms, pointing in one direction. She calculated, and realised they were heading in the direction of the concrete area she'd discovered earlier.

Half bent over, Beatrice followed the arms, keeping her flashlight low, coughing occasionally from the dust. She passed an area with many electrical cables descending from the ceiling. "Must be Google Play," she thought.

The raised arms led her beyond the cabling. She started to hear muffled voices, and switched off the flashlight as she continued to creep towards them.

The noise of voices intensified, coming now from directly above her. She lifted her hand up, and felt the shape of a trapdoor, similar to the one she had lowered herself down into from White Storm's Kabuff.

"Am Morgen! Wir schlagen zu!" one voice, the loudest, called. The others cheered.

Beatrice felt the dust of the secret passageway close her throat. She pinched her nose, but she couldn't hold it in any longer. A huge sneeze filled the empty space around her, just as the voices above her quietened.

Her arm was suddenly wrenched upwards, and bright light blinded her temporarily. When her eyes focused, she saw first 12 steel-capped boots, blue jeans, white shirts, then six faces looming over her, their heads topped by caps bearing White Storm's insignia.

Her defiance drained away. It was too late to escape.

CHAPTER NEUN

A concrete floor, gritty under my fingertips. A pair of steel-capped boots. And in my mind, still, the image of Amina, slight and defiant in the grey evening light. I peer under the door from my vantage point in the chicken shop store room, shivering in the refrigerated air.

"It's time to move." Kev's voice is guttural. "Have you got the stash?"

Heavy steps cross the floor, and someone drops a black dufflel bag in front of the boots.

"It's all in there, thanks to our literary friend and his associates." A snort. "So much for the tolerant left."

I go rigid with shock. Callum is involved in this? Something inside me crumples. All that advice about not getting involved - it was to save his own skin. And all those nights out with the literati, selling chapbooks of poetry and glasses of red wine - a money laundering scheme? I'm roiling with a sense of betrayal, before the next words send me into a spiral of fear.

"And Amina?"

"He's taken care of her too. Told her his girlfriend had assigned her some extra homework. Angela Carter or some bloody thing. Amina won't notice nothing on her shift tonight, with her head stuck in a book. Your slimy politician mate can come back here with the goods."

"Right then. Let's go."

Thank God, I think. It's a risk, being here. And I need to get moving - to warn Amina, to confront Callum, to think about where I stand now.

"Wait a minute. I have to get the chooks on. I'll just grab them from the store room. Flick on the spit, willya?"

The boots come closer, heavy step by heavy step. I'm panicking now. My eyes flick around the store room, looking around for hiding spots. There are sacks of pre-cut chips and loaves of white bread piled in a corner, but nothing substantial enough to cover me. The freezer section with the chickens, right at the back of the room, is the only possibility, but it's too dangerous. There must be another way.

Suddenly, a cockroach scurries across the floor in front of me.

Then another, then another. Acting quickly, I catch a dozen of them in my hand, then push them out the gap under the door.

"Jesus!" That guttural voice is barking now, frightened. "What the?!"

Kev's mate's voice cuts in. "We don't have time for your namby-pamby cucaracha fears, or for pest extermination, or for the chickens. Leave the cooking for Amina. We've gotta roll, or the Ice Queen is not going to be happy."

The front door of the chicken shop creaks open, then closes behind them. I breathe out, relieved not to have been found, stunned and heartbroken by what I've heard. I rest my cheek on the concrete floor. Under the gap in the door, far in the distance, I see a piece of aluminium foil on the ground.

And reflected upon the foil is an image. The flame of the spit, flickering.

CHAPTER ZEHN

The voices above her were speaking in a fast German. Beatrice was too dazed to understand. Her eyes searched the Kabuff, looking for anything that might help her. Slabs of mineral water, teetering precariously. A rack with coats. Those misshapen, wrapped parcels were still there at the back. Squinting, Beatrice thought perhaps she could see some wires poking out from their sides. She shuddered and turned her head. A few metres away Beatrice could see stacks and stacks of books; hundreds of copies of the same book, the words MY STRUGGLE stamped on the spine.

Perhaps, she thought, it was one of the volumes of Karl Ove Knausgaard's memoir, which had appropriated that title from one of history's darkest texts. Beatrice felt a familiar flush of annoyance with the amorality of some contemporary literary fiction. And yet, while she hated to think that Knausgaard's reflections on consciousness and middle-class life in Norway might have been weaponised by White Storm, the alternative was worse...

Beatrice felt herself hauled upwards, her arms wrenching from from their sockets. One of the white caps tied rope roughly around her hands and emptied her pockets, before shoving her towards a corner of the Kabuff. Beatrice stumbled, falling against the books. As she feared, the book was not Knausgaard's, but the first new edition of *My Struggle* which had been allowed in Germany since the Second World War. Even with its careful paratextual apparatus, she feared the worst from this incendiary volume.

"You vill stay here, until ze Ice Queen comes to deal with you," barked one of the caps at her. "She vill not be happy at your incursion."

Eleven eyes and one eye patch glared at her, each one piercing blue. Then they turned away from her, exiting via the Kabuff door. She heard the lock turn in the door.

Darkness.

***

Beatrice was slumped against the copies of *My Struggle*. She had twisted and turned her hands for what felt like hours, rubbing her wrists raw as she tried to extract them from the tight noose that held them captive. She thumped the back of her head against the books in desperation, her mind jumping between the present darkness of the Kabuff and the past flickering of the chicken shop flame.

***

She had no idea what time it was. The white caps had said they would strike in the morning. Had a night passed already?

She renewed her efforts to release her hands. She had to get out, and stop White Storm.

***

Tears streamed down Beatrice's face. She had fled Melbourne, the Chicken Shop, for this? She hung her head, her breast heaving with the pain.

A grating noise. In the darkness, she looked to the Kabuff door. But no light came in.

By her feet, she felt a rush of air. The trapdoor!

A light shone into the Kabuff, blinding her. Instinctively, she tried to raise her hand to shield her eyes. She twisted her head away.

"Beatrice!" a deep voice sounded in the small space.

45

She opened her eyes. She could see. Between her splayed legs, she saw a head. Thick brown hair, deep brown eyes.

"Caspian!"

***

He took her wrists, gently rubbing the marks from the rope which now lay, discarded, on the floor of the Kabuff. A low light played around the enclosed space, the torch on the floor beside them.

"How..." Beatrice stuttered, "How did you find me?"

"Linksphilosophie Verlag," he replied, his eye reaching deep into hers. "Adriana told me. I followed the signs." He ran his hands up both her arms, his eyes never leaving hers.

She felt a sensation running deep into her core. She leaned towards him. Her heart beat loud in the silence of the Kabuff.

***

Her lips on his created a fire she hadn't felt for years. His hands were on her thighs, lifting her dress over her head.

She pulled her liberated hands above her head, feeling the soft air around her body. Her hands scrabbled on his bullet-proof vest, struggling to find a way in. He laughed, low, and lifted the heavy garment over his head. She ripped the shirt open, and ran her hands down his naked chest.

She breathed heavy, as she reached towards his belt.

"Polizeiobermeister Schorle...." she gasped.

He pulled her knickers down her legs, his hands stroking her thighs with a firmness that arched her naked back.

"Beatrice..." he growled into her neck, pushing towards her then pausing a moment. "The plot thickens...?"

"We must be quick, Caspian. White Storm..."

"Ja," Caspian replied, before his mouth came towards her again, their tongues leaping together as Beatrice pulled him into her, her legs crossing tight around his back, her shoes keeping time with their rapidly accelerating rhythm. She lost herself deep in his physicality.

They cried out simultaneously, and held each other for a long moment, their breaths slowly coming back to the pace of the room around them.

The books. The canvas-covered parcels. The wires.

Beatrice pressed herself into his full lips one more time. As she pulled herself away, she let out one last gasp, pushed away Caspian's hot body, and reached for her dress.

"Come," she said. "We have a Buchmesse to save."

CHAPTER ELF

Beatrice strode through Hall 3, Caspian by her side. She reached into the pocket of her somewhat crumpled dress and started rifling through the business card stash.

"What are you looking for?"

"That young woman from the Executive Club. She said she had information for me. It might help us defeat White Storm." Her hand stopped on a white card. Lotte Frankel: International Rights Agent, Translator, and Executive Assistant to the Vice President for Intellectual Freedom. Beatrice looked up.

"Give me your phone, Caspian. There's a call I need to make."

Her fingers pressed the screen with confidence, despite the adrenaline coursing through her body.

"Lotte. It's Beatrice Deft. You said you had information for me?"

Beatrice could barely make out the whispered voice at the other end of the metaphorical line.

"I cannot say much. I am surrounded by them. But your friend is in danger. This morning, when he is awarded the Peace Prize, they will strike. It is not just the White Storm flunkeys, either. This goes all the way to the top. Well, the Vice Top."

Beatrice was delighted to hear that Kurt's publishing career was being recognised by this honour, but given the circumstances, she asked only a single question.

"When?"

"You have ten minutes to save him."

Beatrice flung the phone at Caspian and increased her pace. This was going to be tight.

***

One minute later, they emerged into an Agora thronged with people: paparazzi, smartly dressed publishers, and glamorous public intellectuals. A red carpet was rolled out and up to a bulbous white pavilion formed from interlocking plywood curves and tightly stretched canvas.

"What's happening?" Beatrice heard a voice say to her left.

"I don't know, but the canapés are great!"

Gatecrashers, she thought. They were at every publishing party.

"Technically we, too, are gatecrashers," said Caspian as he shouldered a path through the milling intelligentsia and cultural entrepreneurs, moving towards the pavilion. Beatrice chose not to reply. Her eyes were busy scanning the crowd. It wasn't until they were inside the venue, however, that she saw Herr Weidenfeld.

Seated on the stage.

Spotlit.

**

Beatrice took a seat at the end of a row three from the front, and swiftly applied some lipstick. Excited anticipation sounded around the Agora. On the other side, Caspian had taken up position. He was almost hidden behind the television cameras, but she could see him speaking on his phone, his eyes glancing towards the back as more police officers arrived at the back of the hall. On the front row, Tante Fran and the book club were smiling up at the stage. Herr Weidenfeld surveyed the room, a look of self-consciousness on his face. Beatrice caught his eye, and a smile broke out on his face.

Trumpets sounded. The crowd hushed. The lights, apart from a light on a lectern, and the spotlight on Herr Weidenfeld, dimmed.

The Vice President for Intellectual Freedom marched onto the stage. Lotte followed, looking nervously towards the crowd.

Beatrice leaned forwards in her seat.

The Vice President stopped at the lectern, tapped the microphone twice, took a paper out from the breast pocket of his blue suit. He cleared his throat.

"Meine Damen und Herren," he boomed. "Ladies, gentlemen. I am the Vice President for Intellectual Freedom, and on behalf of the administration, I welcome you to this, the key event of the Frankfurt Buchmesse. Every year, we award the Peace Prize, which goes to a key figure in the world of literature and books, who has over a sustained period of time contributed to the peace, humanity and understanding among all peoples and nations of the world."

The Vice President paused. He shot a cold look at Herr Weidenfeld.

"Past winners include Victor Gollancz, Astrid Lindgren and Jürgen Habermas; publisher, writer, intellectual."

The Vice President glared across the public sphere of the Agora.

"Tonight..." he continued. Beatrice saw Lotte whisper in his ear. A look of disgust travelled rapidly across his face.

"This morning...we break with tradition." He picked up his paper, and looked at it as if in disbelief. "This morning, we are gathered to commemorate the life and work of Herr Kurt Weidenfeld, publisher of Linksphilosophie Verlag, a left-wing publisher known even by Turkish taxi drivers." He spat out the final three words.

Beatrice saw a quizzical expression on Kurt's spotlit face. A hum started in the Agora, as the audience turned to one another, confirming what they had heard. She glanced over to where Caspian had been standing. The cameras were shrouded in darkness.

The crowd fell silent again. Beatrice clenched her knuckles, shifting to the edge of her seat, her muscles primed for action.

"So this morning," announced the Vice President, "we are here to provide the ultimate accolade to Herr Weidenfeld."

He raised his right arm to the air, palm downwards. The gesture on White Storm's Kabuff door.

"Hail Victory!" he screamed.

In the stunned silence that followed, Beatrice saw Tante Fran's hands flutter down into her lap — had she been knitting? — as the members of the book club exchanged glances with one another. Then, a sound of murmuring and coughing swelled from the edges of the pavilion. Chairs scraped on the floor. People stood up. White smoke billowed up from the ground.

"Smoke grenades!" yelled Beatrice, as the air thickened around her.

She leaped to her feet, running for the stage steps.

Above her, Herr Weidenfeld was already a hazy silhouette. Time slowed down. Beatrice noticed four things happen, one after the other.

A shot rang out.

Herr Weidenfeld slumped.

Caspian and six officers rushed onto the stage.

And, quietly exiting the pavilion via a secret door, was a figure that looked very much like the Vice President. As a gust of fresh air blew in, Beatrice caught one glimpse of a mass of white-capped bodies outside, before the smoke closed around her once again.

CHAPTER ZWÖLF

I run back home, and find Callum sitting at the kitchen table with his MacBook Air, leaning back on two legs of the chair, a cigarette in the ashtray. Smoke curls around the kitchen, delicate wisps rising and dispersing in the cool air. My heart is still twisting as I take in every detail of this, the life I thought I knew. It all seems the same. Well, almost all. There's an envelope for me under the ashtray, postmarked from Germany.

I take his cigarette, and draw on it deeply. He shoots me a confused glance, and switches off the podcast he is listening to.

"We have to talk, Callum."

He doesn't deny his involvement with Kev's plan when I confront him.

"I've been telling you for years how hard making a living as a poetry publisher is, but what should you know with your steady teacher's salary." His face is contorted, as he spits the

words out.

"*Writing and reading books is the easy part,*" *he lectures.* "*The difficult part of the circuit of the book is publishing it.*"

"*Yes, Darnton's communication circuit,*" *I sigh. I can't believe we're going over this again.* "*And you're also a hero struggling for symbolic capital.*"

Callum looks up sharply. He can tell something's shifted between us; I've criticised Darnton before, but I've never been sarcastic about Bourdieu. There's a moment when genuine theoretical conversation seems possible, but then his facial muscles shift again, he ignores my words, and just looks at me beseechingly.

"*Now we've got that distribution deal with Allen & Unwin, this will be the last time I work with Kev. Bea, I did it for us. So we can leave this outer suburban neighbourhood and move to North Fitzroy. When I got that funding knockback from the Australia Council because our list wasn't hitting 'equalities targets' I couldn't think of any other way. But you know how good our books are, Bea... I only see excellence.*"

I stare at him, as he tucks a long strand of hair into his Alice band. I take another drag of the cigarette, the nicotine hitting my system, my heart rate rising.

BOOM!

An enormous noise ricochets around the neighbourhood, breaking the tense silence between Callum and me.

For once, it's not just me rushing out into the street. Callum is by my side. "It's the chicken shop," he says, with a thin note of panic in his voice. "I just got an internet message from the lookout guy. I need to retrieve my stuff."

Our feet hit the footpath in tandem, a bittersweet echo of the intimacy we once shared. We hurtle around the corner towards the clutch of shops that is the heart of our neighbourhood. The burger shop. The frozen yoghurt shop. The kebab shop. And right at the end — blackened and pouring out smoke — the chicken shop.

BOOM!

A second explosion rings out and Callum and I reel backwards. But it's just a momentary check. Callum's eyes are steely and he is faster than me. He ducks into the shop.

I arrive at the front door of the chicken shop a few seconds later. I can hear Callum shouting deep in the interior, but the sound fades to a ringing in my ears as I take in the scene. The heartbreaking scene.

Amina's body is crumpled behind the counter. I glimpse Angela Carter's feminist reworking of Bluebeard just beside her and feel a stab in my heart — of course Callum knew that I would recommend this book, of course he knew Amina would love it so much that it would absorb her, blind her to the danger in the chicken shop. When even the best books could be turned to evil purposes, what use were they?

Flames, red orange and pale pale blue, leaping from the fryer. Thick smoke. I realise I have only seconds to act.

"Help, Bea!" comes Callum's voice from the back of the shop, "I need help to carry the goods! We need these for our future."

But my future is clear, and it doesn't include Callum. I bend down and scoop up Amina and run through the chicken shop door, out into the street.

***

Sirens are wailing, and the neighbours are out on the street in force. Amina sits in the back of the ambulance, wrapped in a blanket. She's going to be fine. She's already discovered that the young paramedic woman treating her is an Angela Carter fan, who has promised to lend her more books. I haven't seen Callum yet. The news reporter recording a TV segment out the front of the shop is talking about a corrupt politician, bribes, a drug ring, rival bikie gangs, and more. But I'm done here.

I turn to the elderly couple standing nearby. "Either of you got a smoke?"

The woman passes me one, and I stride towards the chicken shop. I bend down and light the cigarette on the still glowing coals by the door, under the fluttering remnants of the lunchtime specials poster.

The chicken shop will haunt me, I know that. But I will keep moving.

CHAPTER DREIZEHN

Beatrice moved towards the stage, the sirens and the chicken shop still in her mind. She fought through the smoke, rushing toward the chair where Herr Weidenfeld had been seated seconds before the gunshot had sounded in pavilion. She reached for his body, but felt instead a sticky liquid on her finger tips.

Blood.

She got to her knees, crawling across the floor. She scrabbled for Herr Weidenfeld, her eyes smarting from the smoke which still swirled around the stage. She felt the heaviness of a prostrate body.

"Herr Weidenfeld..." she called, her voice cracking as her hands touched the soft wool of his blue suit.

The body convulsed. A cough. "Herr Weidenfeld?"

"Mein Liebchen," Herr Weidenfeld croaked. "Is it you?"

"Yes," Beatrice replied, her heart rising. "They shot you...?"

Herr Weidenfeld coughed again. "A flesh wound, mein Liebchen." He pulled a stash of papers from inside his jacket.

"A taxi driver gave this to me on my way into the Buchmesse this morning. I know it is old-fashioned, Liebchen, but I prefer to read on paper." A bullet had wormed its way through the pages.

Beatrice smiled at the publisher. "We should get you to an ambulance."

A siren sounded outside the pavilion. As the air cleared, she saw Caspian leading the paramedics towards the stage, his phone glued to his ear as they ran.

Beatrice got to her feet, making way for the paramedics who knelt down and got to work. Tante Fran and the book club stood around them, looking down anxiously to Herr Weidenfeld.

Beatrice's eyes met Caspian's, and for a second she was back in the Kabuff.

"Beatrice," he said, urgently, his voice low. "There is not a moment to spare. This action, it is a literal smokescreen. There are bombs all around the Buchmesse. We must hurry."

Beatrice span on her heel, ready to rush towards the hall.

"Wait," Tante Fran said. "Before you go."

She reached into her tote bag and pulled out a knitting needle.

"Take this with you. It may be important."

Beatrice nodded, then twisted her black hair into a simple bun and stuck the needle through it.

"Also, I advise you to start your search at the stairwell at the base of Hall 4. There is a network of tunnels there, which connects everything. The networking of Frankfurt is not just about parties and meetings, but also about infrastructure."

Caspian interjected. "I'll join the SWAT team in the halls while you investigate the stairwell. Take my secondary work phone with you. Now, let's move."

***

Beatrice opened the heavy door at the base of Hall 4. She gripped the stainless steel handrail tightly, hearing a loud noise reverberate around the concrete floor and walls of the stairwell.

BANG!

Should she go up or down? Instinct told her the Kabuff network would be underground, but all bets were off in the labyrinth of the Messe. Google Maps would be no help to her here. She wasn't even sure she had reception.

BANG!

Beatrice peered down the twisting flights of stairs, and glimpsed something - a shoulder? A cap? It was enough. She sprinted down the stairs, grateful once again for the sturdy but elegant shoes from Tante Fran's shop.

Seven flights further down, and a corridor opened up. Electrical wires dangled from the ceiling and cardboard boxes were stacked haphazardly. It was dark here. Beatrice could never remember which screen buttons to press to activate the torch on her own phone let alone Caspian's, but it didn't matter - her eyes adjusted quickly. She stepped softly through the corridor, keeping to the edges.

BANG!

As a third bang ricocheted off the corridor walls, Beatrice paused and sucked in her breath. She was closer now. There was a bend in the corridor up ahead. Beatrice thought of Herr Weidenfeld, of Caspian, of Tante Fran. It was time to confront the evil despoiling the heart of the publishing industry and culture more broadly.

She strode forward. "Herr Vice President, I presume"

The tall, blue-suited figure at the other end of the corridor turned around.

"Ja, you haff found me, Beatrice Deft. Willkommen to the Vorbunker. Those Polizei swarming through the halls will not be able to foil our plan. Every über race has its superman, and even though I am a vice president, today I ascend to become the plenipotentiary, the chancellor, the noble leader who will bring our plan to fruition. No one will ever turn down my writing again!" He held out his hand. On it was a small, wired device with a large red button.

"When I press this button, a chain of bombs will detonate. They have been carefully arranged so that the stands of every organising body of every Book Fair around the world, from Hall 2 to Hall 6, will explode."

He was becoming more and more animated, spittle flying from his mouth and his arms gesticulating as if giving a conference talk. Beatrice eyed the device nervously.

"There will be NO MORE exchange of ideas! There will be no more translations! No more co-published editions!"

BANG!

The metallic sound rang again through the echoing corridor.

"It is time. My white-capped people are communicating with me through the pipe system that connects Kabuffs with hot water for tea and coffee. Four bangs, and all is ready. You cannot stop me now, Beatrice Deft."

Beatrice didn't know if this was true or not, but thought she should at least try. She lunged forward swiftly, pulling the knitting needle out of her bun. Her hair settled back into its sharp cut as she held the needle at the Vice President for Intellectual Freedom's neck.

"Drop the device, Herr Kristoff Wiel. I mean it."

"One knitting needle will not stop me, Frau."

"It is not...just...one."

The voices came from behind Beatrice. A group of formidable women was standing there: the book clubbers, slogan-painters, knitters and shoe salespeople. The readers.

Tante Fran stepped forward and spoke again, addressing the Vice President with a steely glint in her eye.

"It is time for you to leave this Buchmesse. You have done enough harm."

Reaching forward, she swatted the device out of his hand. Another woman came forward and dismantled it expertly. She looked up and addressed Beatrice.

"Alles Gut. I have worked in digital publishing services. I know how to make technology stop."

Meanwhile, two other women had restrained Herr Wiel with wool, and were marching him along the corridor.

"Direct action, sideways thinking, Schwester," said Tante Fran, nodding at their retreating backs. She enveloped Beatrice in a hug, and Beatrice felt the warmth of feminist solidarity swell inside her breast. The dust and noise of the Kabuff network settled around her. The infrastructure of the Buchmesse was sound, for now.

CHAPTER VIERZEHN

Beatrice, Tante Fran and the rest of the book club swept into the Executive Club, their shoes in sisterly synchronicity. The gathered publishers and staff started to applaud, and at the centre of the Club, Lotte stood to greet them.

"Tante Fran, I should have known you and your colleagues would be involved," said Lotte, holding out her hands to the women, who gathered around her. "I've just heard from Polizeiobermeister Schorle. His team has apprehended all the White Storm operatives."

On the badge hanging from her lanyard, Beatrice noticed Lotte's title had changed. "LOTTE FRANKEL, International Rights Agent, Translator, and Vice President for Intellectual Freedom and Inclusion."

"And yes, now Kristoff Wiel is in custody, I've been promoted," Lotte concluded.

Beatrice's eyes flicked down to Lotte's matte-black, embossed heels. This was a woman who knew where to buy her footwear.

"Beatrice, I want to thank you. Join me over here, please – I have more information for you." Lotte gestured towards one of the booths at the side of the Club. "Tante Fran?"

Tante Fran shook her head and patted her tote bag. "We have book club this afternoon. Luxembourg's *The Accumulation of Capital.*" She addressed Beatrice. "We have a Goodreads page if you want to join us virtually. And... I'm glad our letter reached you. It is hard to tell with the postal service nowadays."

"The letter...?" Beatrice had a flashback to her Melbourne table, the ashtray, the day of the chicken shop incident.

"Ja. We had heard of the good work you had been doing with getting high school students to read, so we invited you to the Buchmesse. Thank you for coming."

Beatrice smiled wryly. She had never had a chance to open that letter, but something about the postmark had driven her to impulsively book a flight to Frankfurt when staying in Melbourne had been unbearable. What was the Turkish word? Kismet. She gave Tante Fran a last hug, then settled into the black pleather seats of the booth.

Lotte had procured two black coffees from the Executive Club bar. Without further preamble, she launched into conversation.

"Beatrice, Genossin. You know, perhaps, that the publishing industry is changing in the twenty-first century. No longer do roles sit in well-defined categories, such as editing, sales, marketing, and production. Increasingly we have need for people with... diverse skills. Skills such as yours."

For a second, Beatrice was confused. She knew digital technology was transforming the profession of publishing, but she wasn't a big user of social media, nor was she familiar with XML.

"What skills do you mean? I don't even have a wordpress dot com site."

"I am not talking about digital skills," Lotte said sternly. "I am talking about your capacity to chart a moral path between the freedom to publish and the need to support marginalised voices."

Beatrice thought aloud, hesitating. "Lotte, I never saw myself as the publishing industry's saviour. I've seen the damage books can do."

She took a deep breath, and smoothed the fabric of her shapeless yet stylish dress over her thighs. "But yes, I care about people, and yes, I have started to love books again. Danger does not faze me. And I am a Scorpio. Count me in."

Lotte's eyes glowed. "You know what this means?" she smiled. "You are now a publishing consultant." She handed Beatrice a business card. In thick black letters it read: BEATRICE DEFT International Publishing Consultant.

"Like other consultants, you'll no doubt develop a portfolio of clients. But I would like to make you a proposition. I speak on behalf of a network of Book Fair champions around the globe. We need someone who can troubleshoot when political extremists threaten all we hold dear. And we are hearing disturbing rumours. There is work to be done in Latin America, in China, in Sweden. Will you be our eyes and ears?"

Beatrice nodded, her words "yes, subject to appropriate financial remuneration" almost drowned out by the sudden sound of power tools.

She turned and saw the central screened booth of the Executive Club being cut down, and workmen starting to hack away at the raised platform.

71

"Ja," said Lotte. "There will be change round here. We're going for an atmosphere which is closer to the ... how do you say it in your country ... vibe of the thing? More inclusive. Less fringing."

Beatrice laughed. Australian culture had spread through-out the world. Maybe the next Nobel Laureate in Literature (if it was ever awarded again) was even tending chicken shop in a dusty Australian town.

Just as her mind wandered back to the Melbourne suburbs, more cheering began in the Executive Club. Caspian strode in, trailing a slight limp. As he approached, she saw a bruise on his cheek, and her heart jumped a beat.

"Caspian... what happened? Are you alright?"

"Oh nothing. A storm in a tea cup. They're all in prison now, and the Buchmesse has been cleared of all the bombs."

Lotte shook Caspian's hand. "Thank you, Polizeiobermeis-ter Schorle," she said gravely.

The celebratory mood of the Executive Club left Beatrice, as she remembered what had happened over the past few days, and how much worse it could have been. Books, bombs, injured bodies...

"How is Herr Weidenfeld?" she asked, anxiously, looking between Caspian and Lotte.

"He's resting, but he will be ok," Lotte replied. "It's just a flesh wound. He'll join us at the Literaturhaus this evening. We're going to make his award there. You'll come too?"

A weight lifted from Beatrice. She turned to Caspian, who looked at his watch.

"Time to party?" he asked, a crooked smile on his face. The heat of his body radiated towards Beatrice.

She nodded at Lotte, and returned Caspian's smile. Her body remembered the Kabuff. "To the Literaturhaus!"

CHAPTER FÜNFZEHN

The brightly lit facade of the Literaturhaus spilled its illumination across the street and onto the river below. Beatrice was feeling jubilant, refreshed by a brief shower and a short nap and wearing shiny red heels that had been delivered to her room in the Hessischer Hof "with the compliments of the book club". With Caspian by her side, Beatrice approached the Literaturhaus, a smile playing on her lips and her heart leaping in time with the deep bass beat pumping out from between its vast pillars. As they mounted the steps, she felt the hair on Caspian's arm brush against hers. She let out a delicious shiver in the still-warm Frankfurt evening air.

They pressed through the chatting crowd on the steps, a merry babel of languages from all around the world surrounding them over the robot sounds of Kraftwerk's Trans-Europe Express. Beatrice recognised some of the faces from the Buchmesse as they reached a clipboard-bearing attendant by the door. He scrutinised them both briefly, before his face broke into a flirtatious smile as he addressed Caspian.

"Guten Abend, Polizeihauptmeister Schorle!" the attendant said, winking. "Willkommen. And you must be Beatrice Deft? Please come in." He gestured towards a grand hallway, where people were already dancing to the beats and more attendants stood with trays laden with sparkling wine and ingeniously designed canapés. Beatrice felt her body start to move to the rhythm of the music. Above their heads were hundreds of glass balls with water suspended in them, a conjunction of water and bookishness that thrilled Beatrice with its riskiness while also reminding her of how much she liked reading on ferries, and in the bath.

Caspian took Beatrice's hand and led her inside, picking her a glass of sparkling wine as they passed a tray, before helping himself to another. She shouted over the noise into his ear, "Hauptmeister, hey? You got promoted?"

"Ja. I have four stars now. But my number is still the same," he grinned, lopsidedly.

Beatrice laughed, remembering his bashfulness after the first party. "I'm delighted to hear it," she replied, entwining her fingers further with his, reliving the feel of his body on hers in the Kabuff. "Congratulations!" she lifted her glass, her eyes pouring into his. "Great champagne!"

"We call it Sekt, Deft," replied Caspian seriously, then took a long draught through his full lips. "Mmmm," he breathed, as their bodies both started moving to the beat of Kelis' Milchshake.

Beatrice saw publishers and related industry professionals all around her, dancing, smiling, air kissing and still talking about books, occasionally stopping to exchange business cards. She thought back to her first Frankfurt party, her feeling of estrangement while others enjoyed themselves. But now she knew there was no threat to the Buchmesse, and after several months her body had reawakened with Caspian's. She might even, she thought, pick a new book to start reading tomorrow. As Caspian swung her expertly in and out of hold, she closed her eyes with pleasurable anticipation at the thought of several hours in a bookshop, imagining running her fingers across their spines just as she was now touching the sculptural muscle of Caspian's back.

A microphone crackle sounded over the music. "Is there anybody here from the BOOK FAIR?!" the DJ called out, whipping the crowd into a frenzy as each person lifted their arms high into the air, waving in her direction. Nelly's Hot In Herre blared at full volume as Beatrice, Caspian and the rest of the publishing industry shook off the pressures of the week, and the vexed question of the fate of books more generally.

Beatrice was warm, too warm now, and her long, shapeless but stylish black wrap suddenly felt superfluous. "Do you know if there's a cloakroom here?" she shouted into Caspian's ear, her lips brushing against his tender lobe. He raised a thick brown eyebrow, his warm brown eye underneath it twinkling. "Ja. Of course."

Placing his hand in the small of her back, Caspian guided Beatrice towards the rear of the hallway, where an ornate carved marble staircase wound into the shadowy depths. "So what's the best biography you've read lately?" she asked as they headed towards the top of the staircase.

Caspian's face drew together in thought. "Malala Yousafzai's, perhaps. Though I confess that is a memoir, not biography. The buzz I have heard at the Buchmesse about Michelle Obama's forthcoming memoir makes me suspect I will like that also."

They had reached the bottom of the stairs. To the right, a group of women laughed as they exited an oddly futuristic bathroom, with walls that changed from translucent to opaque and back again. To the left, there was a counter, and behind it, racks of coats. Beatrice strode up to the desk. "Hello? Hello?"

It seemed to be deserted. Beatrice was suddenly extremely hot, flushed in fact. She shrugged out of her wrap, and felt the capable hands of a hot cop on her shoulders. "Let me help you," his deep voice whispered in her ear as he took her wrap. She whirled around and stared up into Caspian's face. "I'll show you how you can help me," she said, nodding her head towards the coat racks at the back of the cloakroom.

In just a few moments they were behind and underneath the coats, limbs tangled and breathing ragged. Beatrice leaned back against a pile of wool and velvet, and Caspian slid his hands up her thighs, parting her legs wide. He shot her a questioning look as she nodded, then gasped in anticipation as his hands eased her knickers off, then slid further up her body, reaching for her breasts. His head replaced his hands between her legs, and she felt the pressure of his tongue begin to circle her. She plunged her hands into his thick brown hair, encouraging his mouth as he explored and licked and circled. A tremor started in her, radiating out from where Caspian's tongue was repeatedly caressing her to her thighs and stomach and beyond. A huge warmth swept through her body and she cried out in abandon.

Beatrice brought Caspian's head back up to hers, and kissed his glistening lips deeply, after tremors still coursing through her body.

She sighed. Now that was stress relief. From high above them, a sound she recognised came floating down: Janelle Monáe, I Got the Schorle.

"I love this song!" Beatrice leapt up, her gauze skirt floating back into place. She ran up the stairs two at a time, her red shoes clicking jauntily on the marble. Caspian laughed behind her. In the grand hallway, the dancing had become looser, more wild and joyful. The crowd exhaled when the song finished and a peaceful hush descended.

Tap, tap. Someone was checking a microphone. Beatrice's head swivelled towards the stage, where Lotte Frankel was standing next to the DJ and holding the handheld mic in her hand. To Lotte's right was Adriana, her black hair swept to the side and eyes dramatically made up. Adriana looked over to Beatrice and Caspian, still flushed from their exertions, and gave a quick conspiratorial wink. Beatrice smiled, remembering how Adriana had helped her get into that first Frankfurt Kabuff. So much had happened since then. Beatrice and her friends had saved the Buchmesse, stopped a Neo Nazi resurgence, and fought off a villain with knitting needles. And somehow, in the process, Beatrice had shaken off the legacy of the chicken shop and rediscovered her interest in both books and physical pleasure. What more was there for anyone to say?

Lotte, the new Vice President, pulled the microphone close to her lips and began.

"Meinen Damen, Herren, und all non-binary friends. We have a leetle unfinished Buchmesse business that must be concluded."

The crowd inhaled. Beatrice noticed people looking nervously at the cupboards dotted around the hallway.

Lotte raised her hands, wincing when the microphone screeched with the sound of feedback and lowering it again quickly. "Do not be alarmed! I am talking, of course, of the awarding of Herr Weidenfeld's Peace Prize."

The quality of attention in the room softened and the crowd parted, creating an aisle down the centre. Kurt, who had been standing quietly against the wall, walked towards the stage: a little frail, but unbowed. The glass balls of water clinked gently overhead. Lotte embraced Kurt before placing a gold medallion around his neck.

Someone behind the DJ started clapping slowly but strongly, and soon everyone had joined in, whooping and cheering for the publisher — this independent, passionate supporter of left wing philosophy, with an open submissions policy and an even-handed embrace of both paper and digital formats — the embodiment of hope for the future of publishing.

Herr Weidenfeld took the microphone from Lotte, and the room hushed again, as he touched the medal at his neck.

"Frau Frankel," he bowed towards Lotte graciously. "I thank you and the Buchmesse from the bottom of my heart. Often my work has felt difficult and lonely, and in the last year dangerous as well." He nodded over towards where Beatrice and Caspian were standing.

He continued. "This is an accolade that I never expected, but I am profoundly grateful for its recognition of what I have been working for my whole life. I said a moment ago that my work has often been lonely, but there have always been comrades to support and nourish my work." He smiled over to another corner of the room, and Beatrice saw Tante Fran beaming back.

"But now, with this award, I feel it is time for me to pass on my work to the next generation." He gestured towards Adriana, who stepped forwards from Lotte's side. "I have been assisted recently by Adriana, who started working with me only a few months after she found safety in our land thanks to the open borders our country offers to those seeking asylum. She has taught me much over the past few years, insight into experiences of which horror I could only imagine, and yet confirmed my belief that cultural interchange is the best way for us to understand each other and continue to work towards a better world. Adriana will from now take over as Publisher at Linksphilosophie Verlag." He took her hand, and raised it in the air as the crowd broke into further cheers. He passed her the microphone.

"Thank you, Kurt, and thank you to this country and this book community, from the bottom of my heart," said Adriana, her voice strong but with a slight quaver that betrayed her emotion. "I will not speak at length as I know we stand between you and more canapés. But I am delighted that Kurt has accepted my invitation to continue as Editor-at-Large at Linksphilosophie Verlag, and I hope in my leadership I will honour his great contribution to literature, and life."

Adriana turned to Herr Weidenfeld, and kissed him on both cheeks before indicating to the DJ to spin more discs. 99 Luftballons pulsed from the speakers as red streamers flew across the room, and the dancing started up again.

Beatrice wiped a tear from the corner of her eye and looked around for the bar. It was time for another Negroni.

CHAPTER SECHZEHN

Beatrice downed her espresso and followed it with a sparkling water chaser, leaving a bright red lipstick stain on both cups. The morning after the night before was warm, with bright sunshine bouncing off the crisp yellow leaves. A little too bright. Beatrice fished dark sunglasses out of her handbag. People chattered loudly in the lobby of the Hessischer Hof, and despite her hangover, Beatrice smiled. After all, she was a Scorpio: passionate, assertive and — Beatrice accepted this now — interested in the lives and culture of the people around her.

The solicitous young waiter with the chiseled jaw stopped by her table. "Breakfast for vun?"

"Zwei," Caspian cut in, arriving at the table after a short walk from the lift. Beatrice lowered her sunglasses and took in his neat uniform, clean shaven face and bright eyes. Overall, his appearance gave no hint of the celebrations that had continued long into the night. The party had moved from the Literaturhaus, to the Irish pub, to the

Apfelwein bar, and finally, inevitably, back to the Hessischer Hof. Beatrice's suite. She pushed her sunglasses back up.

"Danke. We need more espresso. And pastries. And sausage. And perhaps some of that Frankfurter Schnitzel, the one with the green sauce." The waiter raised one eyebrow, then nodded, and left Beatrice and Caspian looking at one another across the white tablecloth.

"Caspian," Beatrice began, just as Caspian said her name. They laughed.

"I admire you so much," she continued, "Your humane political views, your taste in books, your wherewithal in the face of danger, and your unselfishness as a lover. But — "

Caspian's smile was quick and gentle. "Do not say anything more. I understand completely. You have my business card if you ever need to get in touch."

Beatrice grinned in relief. "I had a text from Lotte this morning. I need to meet her at the airport at noon." She nodded toward the wall, where her luggage was neatly stacked. "I just have time for breakfast before I head to the Flughafen." And with that, they tucked in to a hearty meal, doing those choice morsels full justice with honest delight.

***

The taxi wound along the Main river. Beatrice leaned forward in her seat, cherishing every glimpse of this bookish city, which she was soon to leave behind (at least for now) as she began her career as an International Publishing Consultant. Suddenly, her eyes narrowed. There, on the water...was that...could it be...a manboat? She groaned.

"What's the matter?" asked the driver.

"Boats with only male passengers. They're the worst. They remind me of manels." Silently, Beatrice resolved that wherever she went in the future, one of her missions as International Publishing Consultant would be to work against manels of all forms. She hunted in her bag for a notebook and pen to jot this plan down as the car left the city centre and started to speed along the Autobahn to the Flughafen.

***

Beatrice settled in a high stool at the airport bar, a Negroni in hand, sunglasses still perched on her nose. She'd creased back the cover of one of the books she'd been

85

tempted by at the bookshop, an irresistible display which included the latest Nora Roberts, the winner of the New Academy prize in literature Maryse Condé, and a travel guide for creative professionals. Beatrice imagined how this time next year the shop would be populated by the titles that had been the buzz of this year's Buchmesse. The new titles Adriana would commission for Linksphilosophie Verlag, even. Her mind wandered from the page, as she thought about the past few days, all the people she had met, everything that went into the creation, circulation and consumption of books. The annual pilgrimages to the Buchmesse, the continuing international exchange of translation rights, cultures and ideas. Frankfurt lovers.

Beatrice took another sip of her Negroni, smiling at her recent memories of Caspian. She felt the heat of their bodies, as she span the ice around in her glass, her fingers the only cool part of her. The immediate bitterness of the drink was tempered by its sweet finish, leaving her wanting more.

She signalled to the waiter. She observed his broad-shouldered approach and knowing nod as he took her glass to make her another cocktail.

Her eyes drifted to the locations on the screens, which flicked over again. Guadalajara, Beijing, Sharjah, Bologna, New York...

The waiter returned. "You are waiting for Frau Frankel, I know," he said. "She has left this for you." Beatrice took the thick envelope — 130 gsm, probably — and read her briefing.

***

The screens flicked once more. The gate for her flight came up. Beatrice texted Caspian one last goodbye, put the envelope and book back in her bag, and took her purse out to leave a tip for the solicitous waiter.

As she did so, her eye caught a woman facing her on the other side of the bar, unblinking. A strapping blonde. With a shock of recognition, Beatrice realised where she had seen her before. Guarding the first Kabuff.

For a moment the two women's eyes locked. The blonde lifted her glass to Beatrice, then turned back to her e-reader.

Beatrice gathered her hand luggage, and headed for the gate.

***

THE END - or is it

ACKNOWLEDGEMENTS

The Frankfurt Kabuff owes its improbable, remarkable existence to the gracious assistance of a number of geniuses, to whom we offer our thanks. First, Kim Wilkins, whose guidance, instruction and enthusiasm (including an impromptu lesson in Freudian plotting conducted using a notebook propped up against a railing at the Frankfurt HauptBahnhof) has enriched our writing and our lives. To our avant-garde coterie of early readers on Wattpad — including heartclaire (now CillianWendell), fireclaire, SandraDuPrintemps, colounorue, MiriamGrow, SueDriscoll, drdds, skjaldmeyjar, violariveraviolante, LJMaher — thank you for your feedback, encouragement, and the questions that prompted the direction of the manuscript. Thank you to Corinna Norrick-Rühl for expert German language advice including the right German word for a dusty cobwebby cupboard (all errors remain emphatically our own). Thank you Alexandra Dane for sensitive and skilful copyediting — you always knew just how much to query what we were doing. Thanks to Claire Parnell, for providing a critical path and understanding how digital publishing works. Thank you Will Smith, for securing ISBNs for this book. And thank you to all the publishers at Frankfurt 2018 who let us look into their Kabuffs. Funding support from the Australia Research Council Discovery Project scheme DP160101308 and the AHRC Creativity Without Clusters: Overcoming Fragmentation in the Scottish Creative Economy: Creative Economy Postdoctoral Fellowship AH/R013357/1 is gratefully acknowledged.

And, finally, to all the publishers and publishing-related folk at the Frankfurt Book Fair: this is for you.

Watch out for Nazis. And Kabuffs.

Blaire Squiscoll (aka Beth Driscoll and Claire Squires)

ÜBER AUTHOR

Blaire Squiscoll is the author of *The Frankfurt Kabuff*, an autoethnographic comic erotic thriller set at the Frankfurt Book Fair originally available on Wattpad (https://www.wattpad.com/story/164522893-the-frankfurt-kabuff) and now published as Kabuff Books' first title.

When not exploring cupboards and inequalities at book trade events, Blaire enjoys drinking Negronis, ferry journeys, reading the works of Gerald Murnane, and dancing to Janelle Monáe.

Follow Blaire on Twitter: @BlaireSquiscoll

ÜBER KABUFF BOOKS

Kabuff Books was established in 2018, and is an Ullapoolist make-and-do project. For more information, see https: //ullapoolism.wordpress.com/

MAP OF FUTURE NOVELS

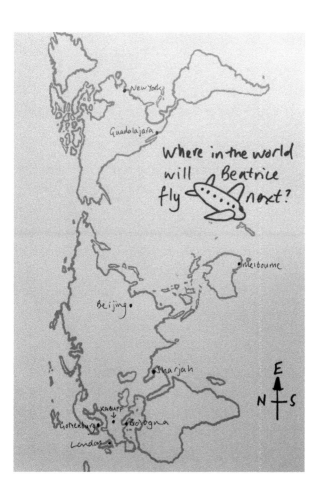

Lightning Source UK Ltd.
Milton Keynes UK
UKHW040204190620
365224UK00004B/1220